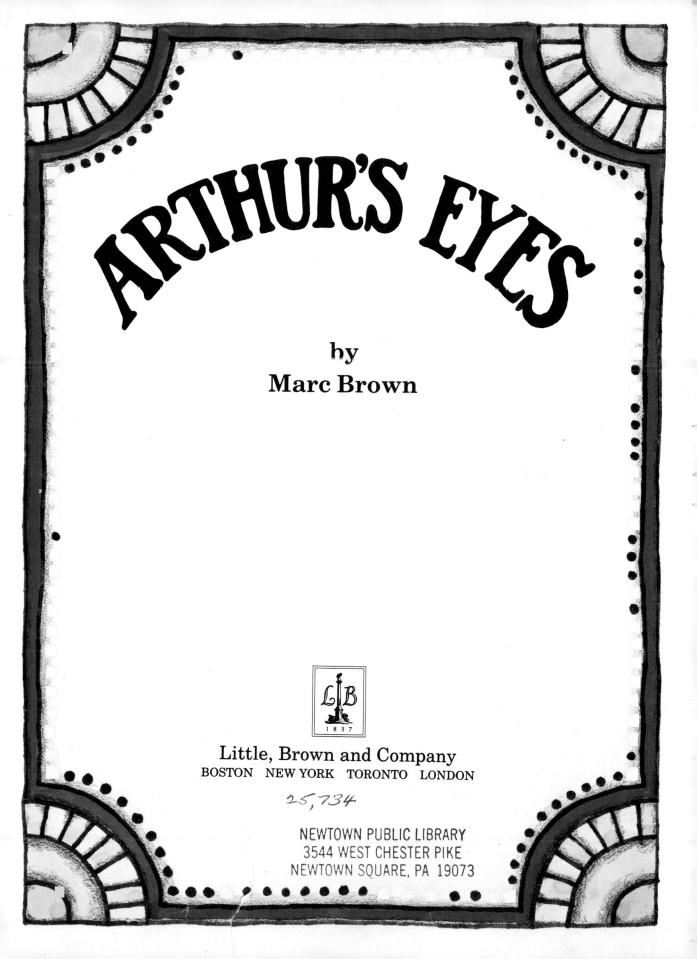

ARTHUR'S EYES

by
Marc Brown

Little, Brown and Company
BOSTON   NEW YORK   TORONTO   LONDON

Library of Congress Cataloging in Publication Data

Brown, Marc, Tolon.
   Arthur's eyes.

    SUMMARY: His friends tease Arthur when he gets
glasses, but he soon learns to wear them with pride.
   [1. Eyeglasses – Fiction] I. Title.
PZ7.B81618Ap   [E]   79-11734
ISBN 0-316-11063-9 (hc)

HC: 20 19 18 17 16 15 14
PB: 20 19 18 17 16

WOR

Published simultaneously in Canada
by Little, Brown & Company (Canada) Limited

PRINTED IN THE UNITED STATES OF AMERICA

This is Arthur before he got glasses.
He looked fine, but he
couldn't see very well.
Sometimes he got headaches.

Arthur had to hold his book so close
that his nose got in the way.
He couldn't see the board.
Francine had to read

Arthur the problems.
"Are you blind?" she always asked.
Francine got every problem right.
Arthur didn't.

No one wanted to play with Arthur.

Arthur's father and mother
took him to the optometrist.
Dr. Iris tested Arthur's eyes.
"You need glasses," said Dr. Iris.

Arthur tried on all kinds of frames.
He chose the ones he liked best.
"You look very handsome

in your new glasses," said his father.
"Everything looks clearer," said Arthur.
His mother told him he looked very smart.

But the next morning his friends laughed at him.
Francine called him four-eyes.
"Sissy," shouted Buster.
None of Arthur's friends wore glasses.

No one in his family wore glasses, either.
Arthur felt awful.

He didn't care if he could see.
He didn't want to be called four-eyes.
Arthur decided he would lose his glasses.

Arthur put his shirt in the laundry.
In the front pocket were his glasses.
His mother found them the next morning.
"You have to be more careful, Arthur.
You're lucky they weren't broken."

That day at school, Arthur hid
his glasses in his lunchbox.
He told his teacher he forgot them.

But now things were harder to see than ever.
When Arthur walked down the hall to the
boys' room he had to count the doors.

He opened the door.
Francine was talking.
What was Francine doing in the boys' room?
"Get out of here!" screamed Francine.
"This is the girls' room!"

Arthur bumped into the wall.
He couldn't find the door.
Now all the girls were screaming.
Out in the hall, doors opened.
Teachers ran out.

The principal appeared.
Everyone was looking at Arthur.
Arthur turned red.
He wanted to hide.
The principal took Arthur to his office.

Then Arthur's teacher talked to him.
"Why don't you keep your glasses
in a case in your pocket,
as I do?" he asked.
"You wear glasses?" asked Arthur.
"Yes, for reading," said his teacher.
He took them out. They looked
just like Arthur's. Brown.
Suddenly Arthur felt better.

He went to his lunchbox and put on his glasses.
In gym Arthur made ten baskets.
Francine made four.
That afternoon Arthur didn't need Francine
to read the problems on the board.

He got every one right.
Arthur could see Francine's paper.
She missed two.
After school Francine asked Arthur
to be on her team.
"I'll consider it," said Arthur.

The next morning Arthur was very surprised
when he saw Francine.
"They're my movie star glasses," said Francine.

"But there isn't any glass in them," said Arthur. "It doesn't matter. They help me concentrate and make me look beautiful," said Francine.

That afternoon a photographer
took the class picture.
"Just a minute," said Arthur.
He took out his glasses.

He carefully polished them and put them on.
"Everyone ready?" asked the photographer.
"Wait!" said Francine.
She ran to get her purse.

She took out her movie star glasses.
"Okay, I'm ready too!" said Francine.
"Smile!" said the photographer.